THE MUMMY'S CURSE

THE MUMMY'S CURSE

MEREDITH COSTAIN

ILLUSTRATED BY BETTINA GUTHRIDGE

williams

Published by
Sundance Publishing
234 Taylor Street
Littleton, MA 01460

Copyright © text Meredith Costain
Copyright © illustrations Bettina Guthridge
Project commissioned and managed by
Lorraine Bambrough-Kelly, The Writer's Style
Designed by Cath Lindsey/design rescue

First published 1998 by
Addison Wesley Longman Australia Pty Limited
95 Coventry Street
South Melbourne 3205 Australia
Exclusive United States Distribution: Sundance Publishing

ISBN 0-7608-1938-6

Printed In Canada

CONTENTS

CHAPTER 1
A SPECIAL PLACE

"Quit pushing me, Vinnie."

"You pushed me first!"

"Stop fighting, you two!" Mr. Bickley's voice was firm. He waved his finger at Vinnie and Ho, directing them to stand next to him at the back of the line.

"Now, I want everyone to be on their best behavior today," said Mr. Bickley to his class, as they stood on the grass outside the museum. "The museum is a very special place."

Vinnie stuck out his tongue at Ho. Ho blew
a pink gum bubble back at Vinnie.

"Don't run," said Mr. Bickley, giving the boys a strict teacher look. "Don't wander off on your own, and *don't touch anything!* Ho, put that bubble gum in the trash can on the way in!"

"This place is big, isn't it?" whispered Vicki to her friend Anna.

"Mmm," said Anna excitedly. "I can't wait to see the mummies."

CHAPTER 2
REAL LIVE MUMMIES

The museum was hosting a special exhibition called "Ancient Treasures," from the British Museum. Mr. Bickley's class had been studying ancient Egypt for months. They'd learned how the Egyptians had wrapped their dead in strips of cloth and buried them in huge caskets. And now they were actually going to see real mummies!

"This way, class," said Mr. Bickley, striding off down a long, waxy-floored hallway.

On the way to the mummy room, Vicki discovered a glass case filled with ancient jewelry.

"Hey, these things are amazing," she said to Anna, pointing to the display. "They must be over three thousand years old."

But Anna wasn't listening. She was staring at a strange turquoise and gold necklace. A man's grinning head hung from it.

"Isn't it beautiful?" breathed a soft voice in her ear. "The ancient Egyptians were very skilled people."

Anna jumped.

"Come on, Maggie," whined another voice. "Our plane leaves in a few hours."

"These things are so lovely," sighed the woman.

She and her husband wandered off to look at some vases. They were wearing matching leather hats and jackets, and cameras hung from straps around their necks.

"Tourists," laughed Vicki. "Come on, Anna, or we'll miss the mummy tour."

Vicki and Anna hurried into the next room, where a museum guide was waiting to give their class a talk.

"Hey, look," said Vicki. "A mummy casket! Look at all the gold on it."

"Don't touch that!" snapped a guard suddenly. "It's mine!"

Anna and Vicki jumped.

"I mean, it's my responsibility," the guard added quickly. "It's very valuable."

He glowered at the girls before moving back to his position by the door. A man and a woman standing near him, dressed in blue overalls, gave the girls disapproving glares as well.

"What a horrible man," Anna whispered to Vicki. "You were only looking at it." She stared at the glaring couple. "Everyone in the place seems mean!"

The museum guide moved over to the class. "I'm sorry if Eric startled you," she said to Anna and Vicki. "He's new. He takes his job of looking after that mummy very seriously. He never seems to take his eyes off it!"

"Maybe he thinks it's *his* mummy," Vicki giggled.

Mr. Bickley shushed them as the guide began speaking again.

"This mummy is very special. She was once a chantress for the god Amun, and she was very beautiful. She is our most valuable exhibit, so we keep a full-time guard in this room."

Over by the window, Vinnie gave a giant yawn. He hated guided tours. It was much more fun finding things yourself. He edged his way toward the back of the class and peered around the corner into a dark hallway.

The only thing he could see was a heavy stone door with a strong lock on it.
"I wonder what's in there?" he thought, moving closer for a better look.

"Not that way!" shouted the grumpy guard at Vinnie. "Can't you read? That's a storeroom."

"Some storeroom," thought Vinnie. The door had been slightly open. The walls inside were stone, too. It looked just like a tomb! Reluctantly, he joined the rest of his class.

The guide led the class into the next room. It was lined with mummies and caskets in glass cases. Ho was the last one in. Arms up and waving madly, he staggered around the room. "Help!" he wailed. "I'm lost! I want my mummy!"

DO NOT
SPEAK TO
MUMMIES

"Ho," hissed Mr. Bickley. "I'm warning you! And I thought I told you to put that bubble gum in the trash. Outside with it. Now!"

Ho walked slowly back to the main room to put his piece of gum in the trash. He didn't care — he had a whole pack in his pocket.

The guide stood in front of a large, well-lit case. "Now this is what we call the 'cursed mummy.'" Mr. Bickley's class oohed and aahed. "It is said to bring bad luck. It was blamed for the sinking of the famous ship, the *Titanic*, but it never really had anything to do with that disaster."

POTTERY

CARTER ROOM

TOMBS

33

"Wow!" thought Anna. She loved to read mystery stories and always managed to solve the cases in the books before the detective did.

"I wish I could get a picture of this," said a soft voice behind her.

"Maggie," a deeper voice grumbled, "we'll be late for our plane."

Anna turned around. It was those tourists again. The woman was staring intently at the cursed mummy. So was the rest of Anna's class. What if the mummy put a curse on them?

"Now, over here," said the guide, "we have some hieroglyphics — the ancient Egyptian form of writing."

"It's a bit like rebus writing," explained Mr. Bickley. "We studied that last month. It's a way of writing a message using pictures."

"Yeah, I remember," called out Vinnie. "Ho got into trouble for writing rude messages in rebus writing."

Mr. Bickley rolled his eyes.

The class moved into the next room to look at cat and baboon mummies.

"Look!" giggled Anna. "A mummy kitty!"

CHAPTER 3
ALARM BELLS

Suddenly, without any warning, all the lights went out. Everyone screamed. Anna grabbed onto Vicki's arm.

People rushed around in the dark. Vicki was nearly knocked over as two people pushed past her on their way to the exit door. "Oh, no! It's the mummy's curse," gasped Vicki.

Anna and Vicki blinked as the lights came back on. Then Anna spotted a leather hat on the floor. She leaned down and picked it up. "Gee, those people were in a hurry," she said, turning the hat around and around in her hands. "Imagine not coming back for a hat as nice as this."

Mr. Bickley was waiting at the top of the stairs. "Come on, class. Line up," he said. "Don't panic. There's no such thing as a mummy's curse. Although, your mummies will curse me if we miss the bus," he added, laughing at his own joke. Everyone groaned.

He counted his students. "Twenty-eight, twenty-nine . . . oh, no, who's missing? Has anyone seen Ho? Trust him to wander off!"

Suddenly, an alarm began ringing loudly. The noise was deafening. The museum guide came running toward them. "It's gone!" she screamed. "The chantress of Amun has been stolen! Stay where you are. The police are coming."

Mr. Bickley's class looked shocked. Something terrible had happened. The curse of the mummy must be real! And where was Ho?

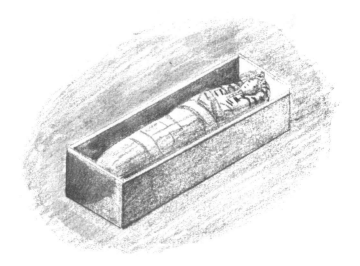

CHAPTER 4

A CRIME TO BE SOLVED

Anna crinkled up her nose. There was
definitely something fishy about those
tourists leaving so quickly. Had they
gone back into the first room to steal the
chantress while the lights were out?

She gently tapped the museum guide on the shoulder. "Maybe I can help," she suggested. "I'm good at solving mysteries. Are there any clues?"

"Only this," sighed the guide, holding up a piece of paper. Anna immediately noticed a familiar sweet smell. "I found it on the floor just around the corner from the chantress's room. It has strange drawings on it."

Anna's eyes widened as she studied the piece of paper. This is what it looked like:

"Quick!" she said to the guide and Mr. Bickley. "Follow me!"

Anna led them back through the exhibition rooms until they came to the storeroom door.

"Try in there," she suggested to the mystified museum guide.

The guide turned the door handle. Locked. She pulled a bunch of keys from her pocket and tried one. The door sprang open.

"Ho!" cried Mr. Bickley. "What are you doing in there?"

"So you got my note?" spluttered a relieved-looking Ho.

"I sure did," laughed Anna, holding up the bubble gum wrapper. "That was clever of you to leave a message in rebus writing."

"Did the guard who was watching over the chantress lock you in here?" asked Anna.

"Yep," said Ho. "I was on my way back to the group when I saw him and two other people stealing the chantress. They were taking it out a side exit toward an orange van."

Ho continued, "When they noticed me watching them, the guard grabbed me and locked me in the storeroom.

I yelled out and pounded on the door, but no one heard me. That's when I got the idea to write the note and slide it under the door."

"An orange van," mused the museum guide. "Sounds like one of our maintenance vehicles. I'd better tell the police. If we act quickly, we'll stop those crooks before they get too far."

She turned to Anna. "Good work. You've helped us save the museum's most valuable exhibit."

"I wonder who the two people helping the guard were," pondered Mr. Bickley.

Anna had a theory about that. But she needed one more piece of information. "Were they wearing leather jackets or blue overalls?" she asked Ho.

"Blue overalls," answered Ho, looking puzzled. "Why?"

Anna smiled. Her theory was right.

The guard's accomplices had been the mean-looking couple who'd glared at Vicki in the chantress's room. They'd been wearing blue overalls because they were pretending to be maintenance workers.

The tourists who'd dropped the hat had rushed off because they were worried about missing their plane, not because they were the thieves.

Anna's eyes sparkled. She loved mysteries. But most of all she loved solving them!

REBUS WRITING

When people want to leave a secret message for someone, they write it in code. Rebus writing is a kind of code. It uses pictures or symbols to stand for words in a message.

Here is how to write "I love you" in rebus.

It's not always possible to think of a picture for a word. When this is the case, add, subtract, or change some letters in the picture-word until you get the meaning you want.

MEREDITH COSTAIN

Meredith Costain finds that although she loves writing, it often interferes with her real interests in life—sleeping, eating, listening to grungy guitar solos, reading other people's books, attempting to keep Boris, her cat, awake, and searching for the perfect chocolate bar.

Her books include *Musical Harriet*, *The Night of the Voodoo Doll*, and novelizations of the TV show *Heartbreak High*. In her spare time she reviews kids' books, works on five children's magazines, and teaches a course in professional writing.

BETTINA GUTHRIDGE

Bettina grew up and studied art in Australia. She moved to Italy with her husband, and after ten years returned to Australia where she began illustrating children's books.

Bettina has illustrated many books for children—books written by well-known children's authors such as Ogden Nash and Roald Dahl. Her first picture book was *Matilda and the Dragon*.

Bettina has had two successful exhibitions of sculptures made from objects she found on the beach. Her special pet is a border collie named Tex.